This Little Tiger book
belongs to:

_____

_____

_____

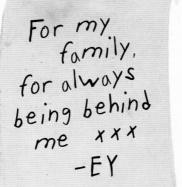

For my
family,
for always
being behind
me xxx
-EY

For Scarlet,
Gabby, Elliott and
Annie, love you
from the bottom
of my heart x
-SS

LITTLE TIGER PRESS LTD,
an imprint of the Little Tiger Group
1 Coda Studios
189 Munster Road, London SW6 6AW
www.littletiger.co.uk

First published in Great Britain 2013
This edition published 2018
Text copyright © Steve Smallman 2013
Illustrations copyright © Emma Yarlett 2013
Steve Smallman and Emma Yarlett have asserted their rights
to be identified as the author and illustrator of this work
under the Copyright, Designs and Patents Act, 1988
A CIP catalogue record for this book is available
from the British Library
All rights reserved

ISBN 978-1-84869-894-9
LTP/2700/3182/0320
Printed in China
2 4 6 8 10 9 7 5 3

CD contains:
1 - complete story with original music and sound effects
2 - story with page turn pings to encourage learner readers to join in

Running time over 15 mins
Music composed by Mark Bates
Story read by Anna Crace
This recording copyright © Little Tiger Press Ltd 2018
℗ Mark Bates

SQUIRREL'S
B'Day
BASH

Friday

Bear's Big Bottom

STEVE SMALLMAN

EMMA YARLETT

LITTLE TIGER

LONDON

Bear was friendly,
Bear was sweet,

The nicest bear
you'd ever meet,

With little paws and little feet...

We LOVE Bear

Come and Play!

His best friends really didn't mind
That Bear had such a big behind,
It made him easier to find —
You can't hide Bear's BIG bottom!

But when they tried to watch TV
Bear's bottom filled the whole settee!
And no one could sit comfortably,
Because of Bear's big bottom.

One day at Squirrel's birthday bash,
Bear turned and made the presents SMASH,

BANG

CRASH

Look out, Mouse!

The pool was emptied with one splash!
Because of Bear's big bottom.

When Hedgehog fetched
the birthday cake,

Which everyone
had helped to make,

Bear made a really
BIG mistake –

He squashed it with
his bottom!

"You've spoiled our day!"
Bear's friends all cried,
And poor Bear felt so sad inside,
He ran away and tried to hide
His clumsy, big bear bottom.

The friends set off to search for Bear,

They shouted,

" Bear are you in there ? "

But then they got a nasty scare . . .

...Fox
tried to bite
their bottoms!

"**Quick**, help us, Bear!" they cried in fear,

SNAP
SNAP

Bear shouted right back, loud and clear,

"I'm trying but I'm stuck in here,

Because of my BIG bottom!"

Bear's little friends
began to feel
They'd soon be Fox's
evening meal!

But then Fox gave a scaredy squeal
And fell back on HIS bottom!

"A Monster!"
yelled the fox and fled.

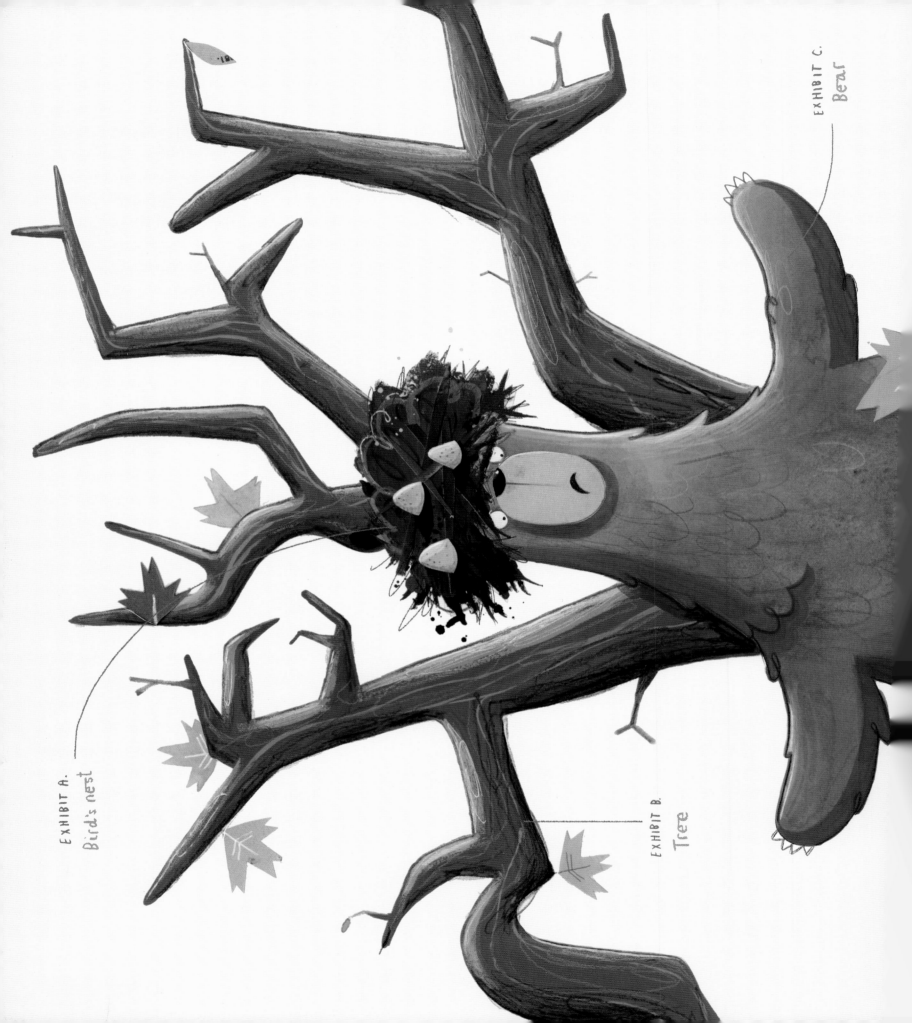

EXHIBIT C.
Bear

EXHIBIT A.
Bird's nest

EXHIBIT B.
Tree

"It's only me!" Bear softly said.
"I've got a bird's nest on my head
And a tree stuck to my bottom."

They helped Bear get his bottom free,
And then he took them home for tea,
And everyone cheered happily,
"HOORAY for Bear's
BIG BOTTOM!"

More fabulous books from Little Tiger!

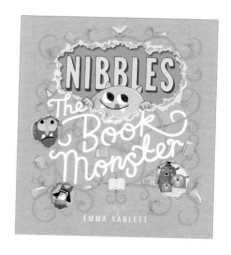

POO IN THE ZOO

Steve Smallman • Ada Grey

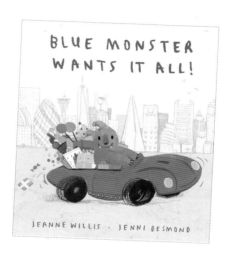

BLUE MONSTER WANTS IT ALL!

JEANNE WILLIS • JENNI DESMOND

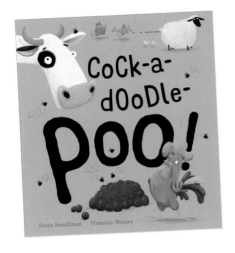

CoCk-a-dOoDle-PoO!

Steve Smallman • Florence Weiser

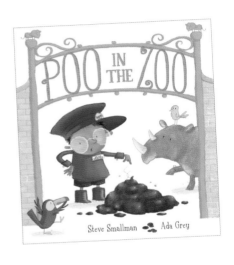

NIBBLES The Book Monster

EMMA YARLETT

FAIRY TALE PETS

TRACEY CORDEROY • JORGE MARTIN

CAN I JOIN YOUR CLUB?

John Kelly • Steph Laberis

For information regarding any of the above books or for our catalogue, please contact us:
Little Tiger Press Ltd, 1 Coda Studios, 189 Munster Road, London SW6 6AW
Tel: 020 7385 6333 • E-mail: contact@littletiger.co.uk • www.littletiger.co.uk